A Note to Parents and Caregivers:

Read-it! Readers are for children who are just starting on the amazing road to reading. These beautiful books support both the acquisition of reading skills and the love of books.

The PURPLE LEVEL presents basic topics and objects using high frequency words and simple language patterns.

The RED LEVEL presents familiar topics using common words and repeating sentence patterns.

The BLUE LEVEL presents new ideas using a larger vocabulary and varied sentence structure.

The YELLOW LEVEL presents more challenging ideas, a broad vocabulary, and wide variety in sentence structure.

The GREEN LEVEL presents more complex ideas, an extended vocabulary range, and expanded language structures.

The ORANGE LEVEL presents a wide range of ideas and concepts using challenging vocabulary and complex language structures.

When sharing a book with your child, read in short stretches, pausing often to talk about the pictures. Have your child turn the pages and point to the pictures and familiar words. And be sure to reread favorite stories or parts of stories.

There is no right or wrong way to share books with children. Find time to read with your child, and pass on the legacy of literacy.

Adria F. Klein, Ph.D.
Professor Emeritus
California State University
San Bernardino, California

Editor: Christianne Jones
Page Production: Joe Anderson
Creative Director: Keith Griffin
Editorial Director: Carol Jones
Managing Editor: Catherine Neitge
Editorial Consultant: Mary Lindeen
The illustrations in this book were done in watercolor.

Picture Window Books
5115 Excelsior Boulevard
Suite 232
Minneapolis, MN 55416
877-845-8392
www.picturewindowbooks.com

Library of Congress Cataloging-in-Publication Data
Williams, Jacklyn.
Happy Thanksgiving, Gus! / by Jacklyn Williams ; illustrated by Doug Cushman.
p. cm. — (Read-it! readers)
Summary: When Gus and Bean go to gather farm vegetables for Thanksgiving, Bean brings his camera along so that he can finish a homework assignment.
ISBN 1-4048-0961-9 (hard cover)
[1. Thanksgiving—Fiction. 2. Turkeys—Fiction. 3. Farms—Fiction. 4. Hedgehogs—Fiction.] I. Cushman, Doug, ill. II. Title. III. Series.

PZ7.W6656Hat 2005
[E]—dc22   2005003780

Happy
Thanksgiving, Gus!

by Jacklyn Williams
illustrated by Doug Cushman

Special thanks to our advisers for their expertise:

Adria F. Klein, Ph.D.
Professor Emeritus, California State University
San Bernardino, California

Susan Kesselring, M.A.
Literacy Educator
Rosemount–Apple Valley–Eagan (Minnesota) School District

PICTURE WINDOW BOOKS
Minneapolis, Minnesota

Be a
Bookworm

4

Mrs. Morrison walked into the classroom. She flipped the lights on and off. It was time for the students to settle down and listen.

"As you know, next week is Thanksgiving,"
she said. "To help us celebrate, I want each
of you to bring in a picture of the one thing
you are MOST thankful for this year."

When the bell rang, the students started filing out the door. "Don't forget to bring your pictures on Monday," Mrs. Morrison reminded them.

Gus groaned. "How am I going to choose the one thing I'm MOST thankful for by Monday?" he asked Bean.

Gus and Bean climbed into the bus.

"If I made a list of everything I'm thankful for, it would be a mile long," said Gus. "I can't choose just one!"

"You have to," said Bean.

"I guess I could bring a picture of my mom, or one of me and you," said Gus.

The bus stopped. Gus and Bean got off.

"Don't forget—my mom's taking us to the farm in the morning," said Gus. "We'll have fun picking vegetables for Thanksgiving dinner."

"I won't forget," said Bean. "See you in the morning!"

Early the next morning, Bean showed up at Gus' house.

"Why did you bring your camera?" asked Gus.

"In case I see something I'm thankful for," said Bean. "That way, I can take a picture of it."

"Great idea," said Gus.

The boys piled into the back seat of the car.

"Everybody ready?" Gus' mom asked.

"We're ready," the boys said.

"Then let's go," she said.

At noon, they rolled through the gates of
Franklin's Farm. Everywhere they looked there
were things to pick—vegetables in the garden,
pumpkins in the patch, apples in the orchard.

"Let's go!" hollered Gus.

"Hold on a minute," said Farmer Franklin.
"Before you get started, I have to warn you
about Mr. T. He'll get you if you don't
watch out!"

15

Gus and Bean froze.

"Who's Mr. T?" they asked.

"Mr. T is the biggest, meanest turkey that ever gobbled," said Farmer Franklin.

Just then, a HUGE turkey strutted by.

"There's Mr. T now," said Farmer Franklin. "Remember, mind your manners while you're here. Mr. T doesn't like anybody. Especially if they're bigger or meaner than he is."

"Billy's lucky he's not around," said Gus. "Mr. T would get him for sure."

Just then, the barn door swung open. Out walked Billy. "Well look who's here," he said.

"What are you doing here?" Gus asked.

"Farmer Franklin is my grandpa," Billy answered. "What are you two doing here?"

"We're here to pick vegetables for Thanksgiving dinner," said Gus.

"I'll help," Billy said with a smile.

"I don't think we're going to like his kind of help," whispered Bean.

Gus and Bean made their way through the
long rows of vegetables. They filled their
baskets as they went.

"Look," said Gus, "a scarecrow."

The boys walked over and stood in front of it.

"Gotcha!" hollered the scarecrow, as it grabbed Gus. Gus was so scared, he threw his basket into the air. All the vegetables he had picked landed in a pile at Mr. T's feet. Mr. T smiled and began to peck.

"Very funny, Billy," said Gus.

"Come on," said Bean. "Let's go look for a pumpkin."

"Look at that one!" shouted Gus. He pointed to a huge pumpkin sitting on a hill. They pulled their wagon to the top and set the pumpkin in it. The wagon's wheels sank into the soft dirt.

"Now what?" asked Bean.

"Let me help," said Billy. He gave the wagon a big push. The pumpkin bounced down the hill. Finally, it reached the bottom. SPLAT!

"Come on," said Bean. "Maybe Billy won't find us in the orchard."

Gus and Bean finished filling their basket with bright, red apples.

"Hey, Gus!" shouted Billy. "CATCH!" He threw an apple at Gus. Gus jumped for it.

SPLASH! Water spurted high into the air as Gus landed on the water bucket. The water made a puddle beside Mr. T. He smiled and began to drink.

Gus and Bean went back to the barn looking for Gus' mom. Instead, they found Billy.

"You guys want to jump in the hay?" Billy asked with a smile. He had moved the hay right on top of a mud puddle.

"Sure," said Gus, as he started running toward the pile of hay.

"Stop!" yelled Bean.

"GOBBLE! GOBBLE! GOBBLE!" shrieked Mr. T. Billy fell right into the puddle of mud. Mr. T looked at Gus.

Just then, Gus knew what he was most thankful for this year.

Gus posed with his new friend.

"Say *cheese*," said Bean.

As they drove away, Gus looked out the back window of the car. There stood Farmer Franklin, waving goodbye. Beside him stood Mr. T, his beak turned up in what seemed to be a smile.

Monday morning came quickly. Gus sat at his desk trying hard to wait for his turn.

Finally, Mrs. Morrison said, "You're up, Gus."

Gus held his picture tight against his chest. He headed to the front of the room.

"I'm thankful for lots of stuff," he said. "I'm thankful for my mom and for my best friend Bean. But right now, I'm MOST thankful for my new friend, Mr. T."

More *Read-it!* Readers

Bright pictures and fun stories help you practice your reading skills. Look for more books at your level.

Happy Birthday, Gus! 1-4048-0957-0

Happy Easter, Gus! 1-4048-0959-7

Happy Halloween, Gus! 1-4048-0960-0

Happy Thanksgiving, Gus! 1-4048-0961-9

Happy Valentine's Day, Gus! 1-4048-0962-7

Let's Go Fishing, Gus! 1-4048-2713-7

Make a New Friend, Gus! 1-4048-2711-3

Merry Christmas, Gus! 1-4048-0958-9

Pick a Pet, Gus! 1-4048-2712-9

Welcome to Third Grade, Gus! 1-4048-2714-5

Looking for a specific title or level? A complete list of *Read-it!* Readers is available on our Web site:
www.picturewindowbooks.com